Cat's Quest

Alison Hawes • **Jon Stuart**

D1344964

Contents

OXFORD
UNIVERSITY PRESS

Macro Marvel
(billionaire inventor)

Welcome to Micro World!

Macro Marvel invented Micro World –
a micro-sized theme park where you have
to shrink to get in.

A computer called ***CODE*** controls
Micro World and all the robots inside –
MITEs and BITEs.

A MITE

A BITE

Disaster strikes!

CODE goes wrong on opening day.
CODE wants to shrink the world.

Macro Marvel is trapped inside the park …

Enter Team X!

Four micro agents – **Max, Cat, Ant** and **Tiger** – are sent to rescue Macro Marvel and defeat CODE.

Mini Marvel joins Team X.

Mini Marvel
(Macro's daughter)

In the last book ...

- Our heroes were on the Big Bug ride.
- A bug chased Cat.
- Max saved Cat using his force shield.
- They escaped ...

CODE key

You are in the Bugtastic zone.

Before you read

Sound checker
Say the sounds.

x   y   qu

Sound spotter
Blend the sounds.

f	i	x

s	i	x

y	u	ck

qu	i	ck

Tricky word

was

Into the zone
Cat and Tiger have gone off to look for the BITE.

4

In a Fix

Yuck!

Tiger ran. He fell.
Tiger was in a fix!

A big bug went past.

It had six legs.
It was an ant.

Ant Facts

Ants are quick.
They run well.

They can pick
up big sticks.

An ants' nest

ant hill

The ant ran up to Tiger.

Yum!

Quick! Help!

The ant got Tiger.
It ran off!

Now you have read ...
In a Fix

Text checker
Find a fact about ants.

MITE fun
Where do you think the ant is taking Tiger?

Yum, yum!

11

Before you read

Sound checker

Say the sounds.

x   y   qu

Sound spotter

Blend the sounds.

y	e	ll	s

qu	e	s	t

qu	i	t

Tricky words

you

my

Into the zone

Look at the title of the story.
Who do you think will get stuck?

12

Stuck Fast!

Quick! Help!

Tiger is in a fix.
He yells to Cat.

Cat is on a quest to get Tiger back. She runs.

The ant is quick!
Cat is not as quick as the ant.

ant hill

Cat tracks Tiger but she can not see where he is!

Cat yells to Tiger.

Where are you?

Cat gets in the ant hill.

Help! My hand!

Then Cat sees Tiger!
He is stuck.
He is in a fix.

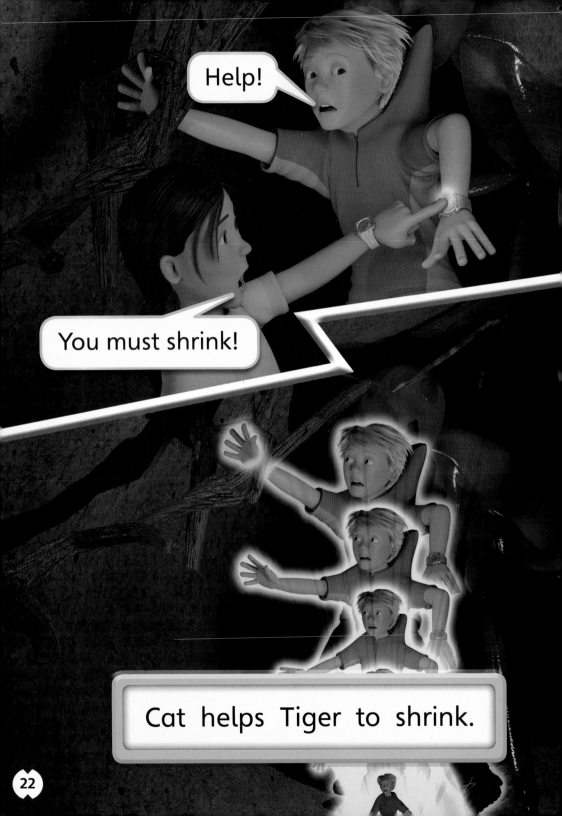

Cat helps Tiger to shrink.